Fairy Ponies

Midnight Escape

Zanna Davidson

Illustrated by Barbara Bongini

Meet the Ponies

Holly

Puck

Bluebell

Pony Queen

Princess Rosabel

Spray

Unicorn Prince

Izagard

Shadow

Contents

Chapter One

Holly sat in the back of the car, dreamily watching the clouds scudding across the deep blue sky. It was the start of the summer holidays, but instead of meeting up with her friends, she had been driving for hours with her parents to her Great-Aunt May's house.

"Why does she want me to stay?" Holly wondered aloud. "I've only met her a few times."

"She wants to get to know you better," Holly's dad replied.

"You'll love it, Holly," her mum went on. "All that beautiful countryside and fresh air."

But all Holly could think about was how much she hated being away from the riding stables back home. Normally she'd spend her holidays helping to muck out and getting lessons in return. What was she going to *do* while she was with her great-aunt?

"Nearly there," said her dad, swinging the car down a narrow lane.

They passed an enormous white mansion that seemed to stretch on for ever. It had a lush green lawn out front, dotted with carefully clipped hedges.

Looking ahead, Holly saw that at the end of the garden there was a paddock – with two beautiful chestnut ponies. She gasped with excitement.

"I'm afraid that's not your Great-Aunt May's house," laughed her dad. "This is it," he added, as he pulled up outside a tumbledown cottage.

It had a little
overgrown garden, thick
with weeds and wild flowers, and
at the end of the garden was a huge
oak tree, its branches waving in
the wind.

As the car crunched over the
gravel, Great-Aunt May came
out of the house to meet them. She
looked much younger than Holly
remembered, with copper-red hair
tied up in a brightly coloured scarf,
and a long flowing skirt that
brushed the ground as she
walked.

"Hello, Holly," she said. Her voice was quiet, almost like a whisper, as if she were about to tell you a secret. "I've been so excited about your visit," she went on. "I've put you in the attic bedroom. I hope you like it. It was my room as a child."

She showed Holly's parents through to the sitting room, then led Holly up a flight of rickety stairs to the attic. Great-Aunt May had to duck her head as she entered, to avoid the low wooden beams. Thick rugs lay scattered on the floor and there was a patchwork quilt on the bed, covered in faded flowers. The room felt untouched, as if nothing had changed here for years.

"It's lovely, Great-Aunt May," she said.

"Just call me Aunt May. *Great-Aunt* is far too much of a mouthful. But I'm glad you like it. I suppose it's a very old-fashioned room now."

There was a faint tapping noise at the window and Holly had the strange feeling she was being watched.

"What was that?" she asked, going over to the window to look.

"Probably just the branches of the oak tree," said her aunt. "When the wind blows, the tips can touch the house."

Still, Holly couldn't shake off the feeling that something had been out there. But all she could see were the fluttering oak leaves and, down in the paddock below, the two beautiful chestnut ponies. "Oh!" said Holly.

"You can see the ponies from here! Who do they belong to?"

"The girls next door – Cressida and Poppy Jones," said her aunt. "Cressida is about the same age as you, I think. Do you like horses?"

"I love them," said Holly, her eyes shining.

Her aunt laughed. "I've always loved them too."

"Do you think Cressida will let me ride them?"

"I *hope* so," said her aunt, sounding doubtful. "You can ask tomorrow. But even if she doesn't, you mustn't be too disappointed." Aunt May paused and looked at Holly, a glint in her green eyes. "There could be other treats in store for you."

Holly wanted to ask her aunt what she

meant; she sounded so mysterious. But she had already turned away, and somehow the moment for asking had gone.

There's something secret about this place, thought Holly. *I can feel it.*

Chapter Two

That night, Holly found it hard to get to sleep. Her parents had left after tea – they'd kissed her goodbye and she'd watched the car as it wound its way back down the narrow lane. She hadn't felt as sad as she'd expected though. Instead she was filled with a strange excitement. Maybe it was the chestnut ponies... *Imagine if I'm allowed to ride them every day,* thought Holly. *I'd learn to gallop and jump...*

Just then, a gentle breeze came through the open window, flapping the curtains so that moonlight streamed into the bedroom. It bathed the walls in a silvery glow, lighting up a tiny painting that was hidden in a nook beside the window.

Holly crept out of bed to investigate, her toes curling into the soft, warm rugs. The painting was of fairy ponies, streaming out from the roots of an oak tree. Underneath, in sloping, curling handwriting, someone had written *The Magic Fairy Ponies*.

"How beautiful!" whispered Holly. There were a dozen ponies, a mixture of chestnuts, bays and dappled greys, and each had a pair of butterfly wings on its back, delicate as gossamer and awash with colour.

Holly climbed back into bed, but she lay staring at the painting until her eyes finally closed in sleep.

The ponies must have fluttered into her dreams, Holly thought the next morning. She'd dreamed she was flying across the night sky, riding bareback on a magic fairy pony, her hair streaming in the wind. Holly gazed at the painting again before breakfast, then tore herself away. "Stop looking at fairy ponies," she told herself, "when there are real ones outside."

Holly wolfed down her breakfast as fast as she could. From the kitchen window, she could see that the two girls from next door were already cantering around the paddock. "Can I go out now?" she asked her aunt, as soon as she'd finished her cereal.

"Of course you can. Are you going to talk to Cressida and Poppy?"

Holly nodded.

"Well, don't be too upset if they won't let you—" But Holly raced outside before Aunt May could finish her sentence. In Holly's mind, she and Cressida were already best friends. *We'll go trekking together,* she thought, *and go to gymkhanas…*

As Holly ran down the garden path she was distracted for a moment by the huge oak tree towering above her. There was something mesmerizing about its twisting branches that seemed to stretch endlessly into the sky.

Suddenly, the sound of pounding hooves made her turn, and she saw Cressida and Poppy had begun practising their jumps. She stepped up onto the wooden fence that surrounded next door's paddock and watched wistfully, waiting patiently

for Cressida and Poppy to come over and
say hello. But even though they must have
spotted her, it seemed ages before Cressida
decided to come trotting up, with Poppy
close behind.

Both girls had ash-blonde hair, but while Poppy's was tied in a bouncy ponytail, Cressida's fell in waves to her waist. They were both dressed in smart jodhpurs and gleaming riding boots. Holly jumped off the fence to greet them.

"Hello, I'm Cressida," announced the taller girl, "and this is my sister, Poppy. Who are you?"

In her head, it had seemed so easy to ask to ride Cressida's ponies, but there was something in the other girl's voice that made Holly feel flustered and uncomfortable.

"I'm Holly. I'm staying with my Great-Aunt May," she said, pointing to the cottage behind her. "You've got such beautiful ponies. I love ponies and I was just...wondering, if,

well, if…you'd ever let me ride them,"
she finished in a rush.

"Can you ride?" asked Cressida.

"Sort of…" Holly replied. "I help out at
the local stables, so sometimes I get to have
lessons. I can trot and I've just learned to
canter."

"Can't you gallop?" asked Poppy.

"Not yet," said Holly.

"I'm six," giggled Poppy. "You must be older
than me, and I learned to gallop *ages* ago."

"Don't be mean, Poppy," said Cressida, and
Holly smiled up at her.

But Cressida's next words were like a bucket
of cold water. "I'm afraid I can't let you ride
them," she went on. "We only have two ponies,
so we couldn't all ride together, could we?"

Cressida was still smiling at Holly, but her blue eyes were like chips of ice.

Then there came a call from the house. "Cressidaaaaaaaaaaaaaa! Cressidaaaaaaaaaaaaaa! Poppeeeeeey!"

Holly peered round the ponies to see a glamorous woman tripping across the field in high heels. "Poppy, your ballet teacher is here," she called. "And it's time for your piano lesson, Cressida. Oh! Who are you talking to?"

"Coming, Mummy," Cressida called back, dismounting gracefully, before leading her pony around. "It's just a girl from next door," she added, dismissively. "She's staying with her great-aunt."

Holly saw Cressida's mother turn and go back into the house, with Poppy cantering across the field behind her. She felt tears prick her eyes, and she looked hard at the ground, trying desperately to hold them back. But as she stared, she saw something fluttering on the grass, just where Cressida had been standing. Curious, Holly bent down to look closer. At first she thought it was a butterfly…

but as she brushed the tears from her eyes, she let out a gasp of amazement. It wasn't a butterfly at all – it was a fairy pony, just like the ones in the painting!

Chapter Three

It can't be, thought Holly, as she went to pick it up in her hand. *I'm imagining it…I'm sure I am.*

But the tiny creature was whinnying gently and struggling to fly away. Holly realized that one of its delicate wings had been crushed.

"What's that?" asked Cressida sharply. She'd turned round and was staring hard at

Holly. "What have you got there? I saw you pick something up."

Holly quickly cupped her hands to hide the fairy pony. "Nothing," she said.

"Show me!" Cressida demanded. "This is *our* land, so anything that's on it belongs to *me*."

"It's just a butterfly with a broken wing."

"Let me see," said Cressida.

When Holly didn't move, she quickly tied her pony's reins around the gatepost, then stalked up to Holly and started peeling back her fingers, one by one.

"Stop!" cried Holly. "You're hurting me!"

But Cressida's long, thin fingers were determined. Before Holly could stop her, she had grabbed the tiny pony and was running back across the paddock towards the house.

Holly started to run after her. She
stumbled, fell and got up again, only to see
Cressida pushing open her front door and
then slamming it shut behind her. Holly
couldn't follow her. What would she say to
Cressida's mother?

With tears blurring her eyes, she turned back, clambered over the fence and raced inside and up to her room. She had never met *anyone* as mean as Cressida, she thought, as she flung herself down on her bed. She pictured her summer holidays with her aunt, lonely and boring, stretching out endlessly before her. As for that fairy pony – could she have imagined it? Had the painting just put silly ideas into her head?

Still, she couldn't resist it – she crept over to look at the picture again. This time Holly recognized the oak tree in the painting as the one at the end of Aunt May's garden. It had the same gnarled and twisting roots, the same writhing branches. As she looked, she instinctively cupped her hands, remembering the feel of the pony against her skin, the tiny points of its hoofs, the softness of its coat. "Stop it," she told herself. "There's no such thing as fairies – let alone fairy ponies."

Holly spent the rest of the day shopping with Aunt May. Every time she thought of Cressida, or the fairy ponies, she forced the thoughts away.

"Are you all right, Holly?" asked her aunt. "You seem very quiet."

Holly just nodded, but when she looked up, Aunt May was watching her closely. "Is it Cressida?" her aunt asked. "You don't have to tell me if you don't want to."

"Well, I don't think I'll be riding her ponies," Holly replied, with a shrug, trying to act like she didn't care. She wanted to tell her aunt about the fairy pony. There was something about Aunt May – her dreamy look, her sparkling green eyes, that made Holly feel she would understand, that she wouldn't laugh at her like other grown-ups. But she still felt too upset to talk about it.

"I wouldn't worry about Cressida if I were you," said Aunt May. "She might have her ponies, but I think you're going to have even more exciting adventures without her."

Before Holly could ask her what she meant, her aunt was putting her arm around her and leading her out of the shop. "Come on. Let's go and cheer ourselves up by buying some delicious cakes."

*

That night, the house must have worked its spell on Holly once more, as she dreamed again of the fairy ponies. They were flying around her, their silky tails brushing her cheek, the sound of their gossamer-light wings humming softly in the warm night air. It seemed so real it drew Holly from her sleep, and as she lay there, just waking, she thought she felt the flutter of wings against her skin. Holly couldn't help it – she opened her eyes… to see two ponies fluttering in front of her, their wings shimmering in the moonlight.

Holly sat up in bed, rubbing her eyes in disbelief. "Am I still dreaming?" she whispered.

"Not any more," the pony next to her replied. She was dappled grey with shining dark eyes, and hoofs that sparkled like tiny jewels.

Holly stretched out her hand and the pony

settled on her fingertips.

"I'm Bluebell," she said. "Puck's mother.

We've come to you for help."

"You can talk?" gasped Holly.

"We can," said Bluebell smiling at her.

"Who's Puck?" whispered Holly, still not daring to believe her eyes.

"My son," Bluebell explained. "The pony you found in the paddock. And this is his uncle, Dancer."

The other pony, a charcoal grey with a glossy mane, nodded at Holly, but nervously kept his distance.

"Puck is only young," Bluebell explained. "He should never have left the Great Oak. We have to help him."

"The Great Oak?" Holly murmured.

"The tree at the end of Aunt May's garden?

I'll help you if I can… I just can't believe it. I can't believe you're real."

"You have to believe it," said Bluebell. "My son could be in a lot of danger right now. His friend, Dandelion, noticed he was missing and guessed where he'd gone. She snuck out to look and saw another girl snatching Puck from you."

"Yes…" said Holly. "I found him on the ground. His wing was broken. Then Cressida took him back to her house. Perhaps Puck's still there."

"We must look," said Bluebell. "You can ride with us. We don't know your world, so we'll need your help."

"Ride with you?" Holly repeated.

As she spoke, a tiny bag around Bluebell's

neck began to glow and magic dust swirled
out of it. Bluebell breathed gently, sprinkling
the dust over Holly. Then she chanted a spell.

"May you be fairy-sized, light as a feather.
Climb on my back and we'll fly together."

Holly felt tingly all over, as everything
around her started to grow. Her bedroom
ceiling suddenly seemed impossibly far
away and her pillow had turned into a vast
pink mountain. By her side, Bluebell was
no longer a tiny pony, but a huge horse,
towering above her.

"What's happened?" gasped Holly.

Bluebell laughed. "You're fairy-sized now.
Quick – climb on my back. Our time in this

world is short. We have to return to the Great

Oak before daylight. We can't be discovered."

Bluebell kneeled down on the bed. Holly

clutched her mane, then swung her leg over

Bluebell's back.

"Hold on tight!" cried Bluebell.

Behind her, Holly heard the flapping of Bluebell's wings as they glided up and up, out of the window and into the night.

Chapter Four

Holly's hair blew in the wind and she gripped
Bluebell's silky mane between her fingers.
The ground stretched out far below and when
she looked up, all she could see were stars,
twinkling in the vast dome of the sky. Dancer
flew beside her, his dark grey muzzle within
reach. "Don't worry," he told her. "You
won't fall. But if anything should happen,

I'm here to catch you."

After that, Holly felt herself begin to relax. She leaned forward and wrapped her arms around Bluebell's neck. Beneath her, Bluebell's legs pounded through the night air, her wings beating in time, and Holly felt at one with the pony, as if she too had grown wings and gained the power of flight.

"The Great Oak, whose branches touch your house, is home to the Magic Fairy Ponies," Dancer told her as they flew. "In its roots lies our entrance to your world."

So the painting wasn't make-believe, Holly realized excitedly – there really were fairy ponies inside the oak tree.

"Only adult ponies are allowed out of the tree, but Puck has always been a naughty

pony," Bluebell went on. "He must have sneaked out and then been unable to make it back with his broken wing. I only hope we can find him again."

"But how will he escape from Cressida with a broken wing?" asked Holly.

"Moonlight has the power to heal our wounds," Dancer explained. "As long as Puck has been able to bathe his wing in moonlight, he should be able to fly."

As they neared Cressida's house, Bluebell saw one of the upstairs windows wide open. "Let's try that one," she said and, silently, they flew in.

It was definitely a girl's room, thought Holly. Even in the moonlight, she could tell it was painted pink. There were pony-print curtains, and in the middle was a beautiful four-poster bed with a big, fluffy quilt. Bluebell hovered above the sleeping girl.

"It's Cressida," said Holly, looking at the long blonde hair fanned out across the pillow.

"Then let's hope Puck is nearby." Bluebell rested on top of the four-poster, so she and Holly could scan the room. To their right was a large wardrobe, with a heavy wooden door. Next to it was a desk, and on the other side of the room was a chest of drawers.

"I hope he's not in the wardrobe," said Bluebell. "We'll never get him out."

"I'll search the desk," said Dancer.

Bluebell and Holly flew around the room, looking everywhere they could think of – behind the curtains, under the bed, in the

bookshelves.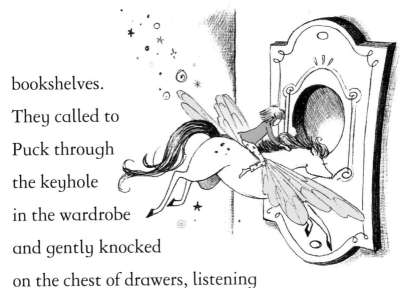
They called to
Puck through
the keyhole
in the wardrobe
and gently knocked
on the chest of drawers, listening
hard for an answer...but none came.

"Where could he be?" asked Bluebell, panic
rising in her voice.

"Maybe we should try another room,"
Dancer suggested.

"Wait!" whispered Holly. "There's a doll's
house in the far corner. Let's check there."

The white doll's house seemed huge to the
fairy-sized Holly, three-storeys high with
a grand entrance and soaring chimney.

"Wow!" breathed Holly. "It's identical to the Jones' house."

"Puck," Bluebell called softly. "Puck! Are you there?"

There was no answer at first, but just as Bluebell was about to turn away, Holly heard a faint tapping sound, lighter than a mouse's

paws on a wooden floor. A moment later,
Puck's anxious face appeared at the window.

"You've come!" he cried. "You've come
at last."

"Oh, Puck!" said Bluebell. "Yes, we're
here to rescue you."

But as she spoke, Dancer whispered,

"Careful! Cressida is stirring! Is there any way you can get out?" he asked Puck. "Have you tried the doors, the windows?"

"I can't open them," said Puck. "I've tried, but I can't turn the handles. The roof of the house lifts off – that's how Cressida put me inside."

"We can't lift off the roof," said Dancer. "Our powers aren't strong enough here."

"We could at least try," said Bluebell. She and Dancer began circling the doll's house, and Holly could hear them chanting a spell under their breath. She gasped as she saw the doll's house roof quiver. For a moment it rose in the air, then it came down again with a thump.

Cressida started from her sleep.

"It's no good," said Dancer, breathing hard.

"It's just too heavy."

"We must think of something," said Holly. "Look – she's nearly awake."

Bluebell flew around the doll's house, desperately looking for a way in.

"What about the chimney?" suggested Holly. "Maybe if I can get in, I'll be able to open the door from the inside."

"We don't have time," announced Dancer. Cressida must have been woken by the sound of the doll's house roof thudding down, and she was now sitting up in her bed, looking in their direction.

"More fairy ponies?" Holly heard her whisper into the darkness. "Where are you?" she said, and began to climb out of bed.

Holly had to stifle a cry. Cressida looked

monster-sized in the moonlight as she walked towards them.

"Quick!" said Holly. "Drop me on the doll's house roof. I'll slide down the chimney. Once we've escaped, we'll meet you outside."

Holly climbed off Bluebell's back and clung to the chimney. A moment later Dancer and Bluebell made for the window, but they were too late – Cressida had seen them.

"I knew it!" she cried, lunging at them. "I knew there must be more of you." She tried to grab them, but they swerved past her, heading for the open window. Before her fingers could close around them, they were out in the night sky once more.

"Well, if I can't have you, you're not coming back in," said Cressida, closing the window on them. "I don't want you trying to rescue my fairy pet."

She spun back to the doll's house.

Oh no! thought Holly, as she realized the time had come for her to climb down the chimney. She peered into what seemed like an endless black tunnel. *I can't do it!* she thought. But Cressida was walking back towards the doll's house, her enormous hands held out

before her." *Imagine what those fingers could do to me now*, she thought, and plucking up the last of her courage, she leaped down the chimney.

Chapter Five

Down, down, down Holly fell. The inside of the
chimney was smooth and hard, its walls like a
slippery chute. She sped down it, whizzing
faster and faster. At the bottom, the chimney
curved round, and with a whoosh she shot out
into the grate. Puck neighed in surprise and
Holly fell forward, knocking over a heavy iron
fireguard that clattered to the floor.

"What was that?" hissed Cressida. Her face loomed up to the window, until all Holly could see was a huge eyeball. She crept back into the fireplace, hiding behind a fire screen.

"What was all that noise for?" Cressida said to Puck, her voice booming in Holly's ear. Puck just looked at her dumbly. "You can't speak, can you?" Cressida went on. "You're just an animal, even if you are a fairy one. Well, don't make any more noise tonight. I'm going back to bed."

As soon as Cressida had gone, Holly crept out from her hiding place. "Hello," Holly said shyly, keeping her voice to a whisper. "I'm Holly. Bluebell and Dancer brought me here, so I could help you escape. How's your wing? Is it better?"

"Yes, it's mended," Puck replied. "There was a chink in Cressida's curtains, so I was able to bathe my wing in moonlight and heal it." Holly noticed he hung back, keeping his distance. "You're the first human I've ever spoken to," he added.

"I promise I won't hurt you," said Holly. "Anyway, I can't! I'm only fairy-sized. Your mother sprinkled me with fairy dust." But even though she spoke as gently as she could, Puck stayed hidden in the shadows, refusing to come any closer. "What is it?" asked Holly. "Are you afraid of me?"

"It's not that," said Puck. He paused for a moment. "Promise you won't laugh?"

"I promise."

"Okay," Puck said finally, and trotted towards her.

Holly had to stifle a giggle. Puck's mane and tail were stiff with glittery clips and bows. Pink ribbons had been threaded through his mane and tail and, funniest of all, he had a frilly cap fastened with a big bow. From his outraged expression, Holly could tell he had been trying to shake it off.

"Look what Cressida did to me!" Puck exclaimed. "It was awful. I couldn't fly away because my wing hadn't mended then. She said she was going to keep me as a pet and call me Posy."

"Well," said Holly, choking back her laughter, "I think you look lovely, Posy."

For a moment Puck looked furious, then he grinned at Holly, finally seeing the funny side. "Will you take them out for me?" he pleaded.

Holly undid the clips and smoothed out his plaits, admiring his silky brown mane and tail and his glittering wings. "Now we must go," she said, heading for the front door. "We both need to get back before day breaks."

She pushed at the door, turning the handle this way and that, but it wouldn't budge. "It seems to be sealed shut," she said. "I don't think Cressida's ever played with this doll's house. It just won't open."

"There's another door at the back. Try that one," suggested Puck.

But like the first, it wouldn't open. Starting to feel scared, Holly went round the doll's house, trying the latches on all the windows. Then she ran back to the first door, turning the handle again, desperately trying to open it.

"What are we going to do?" she cried. "The only way out is the roof and only Cressida can lift that off…" Thoughts raced through her mind. What would Aunt May do in the morning, when she saw Holly's empty bed? Even worse, what would Cressida do if she found her, fairy-sized, trapped inside the doll's house?

"We'll be stuck here for ever," said Puck. He sank down onto the floor, hanging his head. "It's all my fault. I should never have left the Great Oak. I just wanted to see what your world was like. And now we'll never get out of here…"

Chapter Six

Holly forced herself to be calm so she could comfort Puck. "Of course we'll get out," she said firmly. "And I don't blame you for sneaking out. It must be so dark and gloomy inside that tree."

Puck looked at Holly in astonishment. "I forgot," he said at last. "You don't know anything about our world, do you?"

"Your world?" Holly repeated. "What do you mean?"

"There's a whole world inside the Great Oak," Puck explained. "It's called Pony Island and it stretches all the way from the Sunlit Sea to Rainbow Shore. There are the Magic Pony Pools where we go to bathe, beautiful meadows filled with flowers and a river that sings as it flows. I only came out for an adventure."

"Really?" gasped Holly, round-eyed with wonder. "I *wish* I could go there."

"People aren't allowed," Puck explained, "unless they take the Fairy Pony Secret Promise."

"Can't I take it? I'd do anything to go."

"The Pony Queen decides who can take the

promise," Puck replied, "but I've only ever heard of one human who came to Pony Island, and that was years ago."

"Oh! If only the Pony Queen would allow me to go too. It sounds like a dream," said Holly. "We'll get you home," she went on. "There has to be a way."

"I know!" said Puck, his eyes gleaming. "We've just got to get Cressida to lift off the roof again. She won't know my wing's mended and we'll fly straight out."

"But how will we wake her? She'll never hear us if we shout."

"Watch this," cried Puck. He reared up on his hind legs and aimed his flailing hoofs at the kitchen table. It wasn't plastic, like the doll's house furniture Holly was used to, but

was made of real wood and came crashing
to the floor.

"Let's make some noise!" said Puck,
grinning.

Holly and Puck raced around the doll's
house, banging pots and pans together, tipping
over furniture and rapping on the windows.

But Cressida didn't stir.

"Come on, Holly!" cried Puck, neighing as loudly as he could, while Holly sent doll's house ornaments tumbling down the stairs.

"What's going on?" Cressida murmured, sitting up sleepily. She climbed out of bed and stumbled over to the doll's house.

"Hurry, Holly! Onto my back!" cried Puck, as Cressida began to take off the roof.

Holly leaped onto Puck and with a flap of his wings, they flew up and out of the doll's house. Puck brushed past Cressida, but for a moment she was too stunned to move. "Come back!" she cried.

Puck headed for the bedroom window, while Cressida snatched at them with her hands. Through a gap in the curtains, Holly could see Bluebell and Dancer waiting for them outside. "No, Puck!" she cried. "The window's shut. We can't get out that way."

Puck turned as fast as he could, only to collide with Cressida's flailing fingers. He managed to zigzag past her and began spiralling up, just out of Cressida's reach.

"Where now?" Puck asked.

"The door," Holly whispered in his ear. "Quick!"

As if reading her thoughts, Cressida was there before them, pushing at the door as hard as she could. Puck headed for the narrowing gap between the door and the wall, determined to make it. Holly held her breath — they were going to be crushed, she was sure. But with only a split-second to spare, Puck shot through the narrow gap, just before the door slammed behind them.

Puck hovered a moment in mid-air, looking to see where they could go next, but Cressida gave them no time. She flung herself out of her bedroom, and began swatting at them with a jumper, forcing Puck to weave from side to side. By his panting breath, Holly could tell he was beginning to tire.

"Look, there's an open window up ahead," she called, "at the top of the attic stairs. Do you think you can make it?"

With a final effort of his tired wings, Puck climbed high in the air. Cressida threw herself up the stairs and made one desperate last grab for them. This time her fingers closed around Puck's tail.

"Do something, Holly!" cried Puck, as he felt himself wrenched backwards through the air.

Holly turned to swipe at Cressida's fingers, but it was useless. What could she do now she was fairy-sized?

Chapter Seven

At that moment Cressida looked up, staring straight into Holly's face. "It's you!" she gasped. "B-b-but look at you! You're not a fairy, are you?" In her shock, she let go of Puck's tail and he didn't waste a second. Beating his wings as hard as he could, he headed for the open window. The next moment they were flying to their freedom in the cool night air.

Cressida's shouts came ringing after them. "I'll get you!" she called. "Even if it's the last thing I do…"

"Don't stop, Puck," said Holly, urging him on. "We're nearly away!"

They came to rest in the branches of the oak tree. Holly clambered off Puck's back, just as Bluebell and Dancer

came sailing round from the other side of the house. "Over here!" called Holly.

"Thank goodness you're alright," cried Bluebell, landing beside them. She gently nuzzled Puck, and Holly could see the relief in her eyes that they were safely out of Cressida's clutches.

"Thank you, Holly, for all you've done," said Dancer, quietly.

"But Cressida *saw* me," Holly burst out. "And now she knows about the fairy ponies. What if she tells people?"

"Don't worry," said Dancer. "When we get back to Pony Island, my powers will be restored, and I can cast a Spell of Forgetfulness over Cressida. She'll remember nothing of this night – and nothing of the fairy ponies."

"Now climb on my back, Holly," said Bluebell. "It's time for us to go. Are you ready to fly again, Puck?"

"Of course," said Puck. "You know, I wasn't scared of Cressida!"

Holly smiled at him and swung herself onto Bluebell's back. "Are you…taking me home now?" she asked, longing to go to Pony Island, but not daring to ask.

"Of course," said Bluebell, and to Holly's disappointment they headed straight for her bedroom window.

Bluebell landed gently on Holly's bed, then as soon as Holly had dismounted she flew around her, sprinkling her with magic dust and chanting another spell.

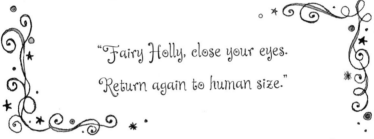

"Fairy Holly, close your eyes.
Return again to human size."

Holly felt the same tingling feeling, only this time everything in her bedroom seemed to shrink as she grew to her full size again.

"We must go now," said Bluebell. "But I can't thank you enough."

"Goodbye, Holly," Puck called.

Holly watched them wistfully from her window until they were just specks in the distance, only turning when she heard her bedroom door creak open.

"I thought I heard a noise," said her great-aunt. "Can't you sleep, Holly?"

Holly didn't know what to say. "Um, no...I couldn't, I..."

Aunt May took in her windswept hair and dirty feet and smiled. "Perhaps you've been having an adventure?" she said. "I expect you'll be wanting to go to bed now." Still smiling, she went out, softly closing the door behind her.

What a strange thing to say, Holly thought. *It's not as if Aunt May could know where I've been...*

Before she went back to bed, Holly couldn't resist looking at the picture on the wall one last time. As she looked, she noticed a figure in the painting that she hadn't spotted before, peeping out from behind the tree. It was a little girl with copper-red hair in a long white nightdress. She was so faint, Holly couldn't quite make out her face. *Is that Aunt May?*

Holly wondered. Her mind was buzzing. *Had Aunt May ever been to Pony Island? Would she, Holly, ever get to go there?*

Filled with sadness that she might never see the fairy ponies again, Holly couldn't get back to sleep, however hard she tried. As she tossed and turned in her bed, she didn't hear the whisper of wings as Puck fluttered back through her bedroom window. It was only when he landed on her bed, his hoofs lightly tapping the wooden frame, that Holly realized she wasn't alone.

"My mum's spoken to the Pony Queen," said Puck excitedly. "She wants to thank you for saving me. Will you come to Pony Island, and take the Secret Promise?"

"Wow!" cried Holly, sitting up in

excitement. "Of course I'll come."

"Then let's go!" said Puck. "We must hurry, it's nearly dawn."

Puck sprinkled her with magic dust and chanted the spell, and the next moment Holly was fairy-sized and riding Puck, taking to the sky once more. On the horizon, Holly could just see the rosy-fingered light of dawn, but she didn't feel tired. Her whole body was alive with excitement.

Puck turned and looked at Holly, as if sensing her delight. "Pony Island here we come!" he said, grinning at her.

Ahead of them, the Great Oak's branches waved as if in welcome.

"Put your arms around my neck, Holly,"
Puck told her.

A moment later, Puck dived down steeply
as he headed towards the roots of the oak tree.
Holly had to cling on tightly, wrapping her
arms around Puck's
neck, her face
pressed against
the silky smoothness
of his coat.

Just as Holly
thought they would
crash to the ground, Puck
hovered for a moment so that his
hoofs gently brushed the ground and
then, in one seamless move, they were
galloping down a narrow tunnel that

wound its way between the oak tree's roots.

As the tunnel closed around them, darkness descended, but for a stream of diamond-bright, sparkling light that showed the way. Holly loosened her grip on Puck's neck and allowed herself to relax into the rhythm of his galloping hoofs.

"Just to think," Holly said to herself, "at the end of this tunnel is Pony Island – a land full of magical ponies." *I can't believe this is really happening.* She felt ripples of nervous excitement in her tummy – what would Pony Island be like? Could it be as beautiful as Puck had described?

As they turned a corner, she saw a glimmer of light, and then, as they galloped nearer, she had her first view of Pony Island...

Chapter Eight

A meadow, filled with flowers, stretched out before her. Beyond the meadow was a line of gently sloping hills, and in the far distance, snow-capped mountains rose up into a bright blue sky. The scent of flowers filled the air and butterflies danced around her. Puck soared above the carpet of flowers, and Holly had to pinch herself to make sure she wasn't dreaming.

"So," said Puck, swooping through the sweet-scented air, "what do you think of Pony Island?"

"It's beautiful," breathed Holly. "Is it always daytime here?" she asked, feeling the warmth of the sun on her skin.

"Oh no," said Puck. "But our night and day happen at different times to your world."

Holly gazed and gazed at the view, never wanting this moment to end.

"Are you excited about meeting the Pony Queen?" Puck asked.

"I am...only now I'm here, I feel nervous too."

"You don't need to be scared," said Puck. "She's very kind – but powerful and mysterious, too. Whenever I see her, I can't help thinking she knows about everything I've done."

They flew over the wild flower meadow, through a little wood and came out into a beautiful valley, with a river running through it. Next to the riverbank stood a cluster of

ponies. Puck fluttered down beside Bluebell.
As Holly slid off Puck's back,
she smiled shyly at the
other ponies,
then gasped.

Coming through the air towards her was
the most beautiful pony she had ever seen.
Her wings shimmered as if flecked by precious
jewels. She wore a crown of flowers on her
head and a train of butterflies danced in her
wake. A halo of golden dust surrounded her,
sparkling whenever she moved. *The Pony
Queen*, Holly whispered to herself.

"Welcome to Pony Island, Holly," she said,
her voice like the sound of tinkling bells. "It's
an honour to have you here. Bluebell has told
me of your bravery. Now, are you ready to
take the Fairy Pony Secret Promise?"

For a moment Holly felt too dazzled by her
beauty to speak, but a gentle nudge from
Puck brought the words back to her lips. "I
am! I am!" she said. "I'd do anything to be
allowed to come here."

"It's our way of saying thank you, for all
your help when Puck was in trouble," the
Pony Queen went on. "But you must also
understand that the promise you are about to
take is a serious one. It's very important that
we remain secret from your world, so you must
never speak of us to another human being.

Do you feel able to make that promise?"

"Yes, Your Majesty, I do," said Holly. She had never felt so sure of anything in her life.

"Good." The Pony Queen smiled. "Then let the ceremony begin!" At these words, all the ponies on the riverbank stamped their hoofs on the ground four times. Then the Pony Queen spoke to Holly in a low, whispering chant.

"You saved a pony by cover of night,
You followed a trail of sparkling light,
That led through the roots of the magic tree –
Welcome, Holly, what do you see?
A land beneath another sky,
Where ponies laugh and play and fly.
Promise you will never tell
Where the fairy ponies dwell."

"I promise," said Holly, solemnly.

The ponies then stamped their hoofs four more times. A blue bird, azure as the sky, fluttered down and presented the Pony Queen with a tiny silver bell on a ribbon necklace. The Pony Queen took it between her teeth and passed it over Holly's head. "This bell is a sign that you have taken the Secret Promise, and will do all you can to protect Pony Island. It is also a sign of our friendship. Ring it before you come to Pony Island, and a pony will be there to greet you."

"Thank you," said Holly. "I'll wear it *always*," she added, slipping it under her pyjama top so it was safely hidden from view. The ribbon felt light and silky next to her skin.

"Now for the last part of the ceremony,"
said the Pony Queen. She threw back her
head and let out a long, loud whinny. In reply,
the air suddenly became alive with ponies
flying across the sky. There were chestnut
ponies and bays, piebalds and dappled greys,

all fluttering their butterfly wings in the sunlight.

"Welcome, Holly, our new friend!" they said, and from baskets around their necks they cast down hundreds of flower petals, which sailed through the sky like a falling rainbow.

Holly felt tears prick her eyes as all the ponies gathered around her, eager to greet her and make her feel at home.

"Thank you," was all she could say.

"Now, it is time for you to return to your own world," said the Pony Queen. "It will be morning there soon. But you can come again. You are always welcome here, Holly." As she spoke, she passed Holly a tiny bag of magic dust.

"When you want to come to Pony Island, stand by the Great Oak and sprinkle yourself with this dust," the Pony Queen explained. "It will make you fairy-sized. Inside the bag there is also a magical oak leaf. Keep it somewhere secret, as on it are written the words to the spells that  will allow you to pass in and out of the Great Oak."

"I'll come whenever I can," said Holly. "Although I'll have to be careful, so Aunt May doesn't find out where I am," she added, almost to herself.

"You don't have to worry about your Aunt May," said the Pony Queen, smiling.

Holly looked up, a question in her eyes.

"Didn't you guess? Your great-aunt used to come here too, when she was a little girl."

"She did?" gasped Holly. And then she remembered – the painting in her room... the mysterious things Aunt May had said to her...

"You must never mention us to her though," the Pony Queen went on, as if reading Holly's thoughts. "Even though she knows about us, she is an adult now. That means we are no longer visible to her, and the Secret Promise you have both taken means you cannot talk about us. You never know who might be listening. Besides, your great-aunt last came here so long ago, we are probably more like a dream to her now."

"It must seem like a beautiful dream though," said Holly. "I'm sure she hasn't forgotten you." She knew now why Aunt May had invited her to stay – she had wanted Holly to discover the fairy ponies for herself.

"I must attend to other matters now," said the Pony Queen, rising up into the air on her shimmering wings. "Puck will take you to the entrance to the Great Oak. I'm sure I'll see you again soon, Holly."

Holly waved goodbye to her, then climbed onto Puck's back. They flew in silence to the oak tree, each wrapped in their own thoughts.

"Thank you, Puck," said Holly, wrapping her arms around his neck, her face buried in his silky-soft mane. "I can't wait to come back again. But how will I know where to find you?"

"Just ring your silver bell when you reach the Great Oak," Puck replied, "and I'll make sure I'm waiting for you on the other side."

Holly smiled in delight, reaching for the magical bell beneath her top. "Wow!" she said. "I know we're going to have so many amazing adventures together."

Holly gave Puck one last quick hug, before she turned and ran back down the narrow tunnel towards the dawn light, and her own world. When she reached the entrance,

she looked down at the sparkly writing on the leaf and said the words of the spell…

"I'm fairy Holly, I close my eyes,
Stretch my arms, reach for the skies,
Magic me back to my human size."

She felt her body begin to tingle all over. Stars danced before her eyes and when she opened them she was no longer fairy-sized, but a human-sized girl again, standing next to the gnarled old oak tree.

Ahead, she could see her great-aunt's cottage, cosy and welcoming. Holly raced up the garden, brushing through the dewy grass, and gently pushed open the wooden door.

Before she went inside, she took one last look back. The sun was rising, its first rays of light bathing the oak tree in a golden glow, its branches reaching up majestically into the rose-tinted sky.

Just to think, there's a whole world inside that tree. Pony Island. A world more magical than I could ever have dreamed. And I can't wait to go back!

Edited by Stephanie King and Becky Walker

Designed by Brenda Cole

Reading consultant: Alison Kelly,
University of Roehampton

First published in 2014 by Usborne Publishing Ltd.,
Usborne House, 83-85 Saffron Hill, London EC1N 8RT, England.
www.usborne.com